crogo

skyrus

BAKUGAN
BATTLE BRAWLERS

A BRAND-NEW BRAWL

BY TRACEY WEST

SCHOLASTIC INC.

NEW YORK   TORONTO   LONDON   AUCKLAND   SYDNEY

MEXICO CITY   NEW DELHI   HONG KONG   BUENOS AIRES

ISBN-13: 978-0-545-13123-0
ISBN-10: 0-545-13123-5

© Spin Master Ltd/Sega Toys.

12 11 10 9 8 7 6 5 4 3 2   9 10 11 12 13 14/0

Cover art by Tom LaPadula
Printed in the U.S.A.
First printing, June 2009

The warm sun beat down on Bakugan Valley. Tall cliffs towered over a wide, flat plateau of orange sand. Tumbleweeds kicked up dust as they rolled across the ground.

Two Bakugan brawlers faced off against each other in this deserted battleground. One was a teenage girl with white-blonde hair and big, blue eyes. The other was a teenage boy with straight yellow hair topped by a white baseball cap with a black brim and lightning bolt design. Freckles dotted the bridge of his nose.

The boy, Billy, called out to his opponent. "Hey, Julie! I'm gonna clean the floor with you, and you want to know why? Because me and my Bakugan are a precision team! And we're in the top twenty of the world-ranking Bakugan players. Yeah!"

Julie smiled, happy for her old friend. She and Billy had known each other since they were little kids. They were older now, and they both had something in common — they loved to play Bakugan.

"Wow, cool! Is that really true, Billy?" Julie asked. Every time a Bakugan battle was held, the results of the game were recorded on the Bakugan website. The webmaster, a guy named Joe, calculated the rankings. Only the best players could make it into the top twenty.

"You bet your Baku-pod!" Billy replied. He looked down at the brown Bakugan ball in his hand. "Am I right, Cycloid, or what?"

The Bakugan ball popped open to reveal a warrior with one big eye and a blunt horn growing from his forehead.

"Oh yeah, you said it!" Cycloid replied in a gruff voice. He sounded like a dynamic pro wrestler. "Together, you and me are uuuuuuunstoppable!"

He twisted his head to look at Julie. "So you might as well go run home to your mama!"

Julie's blue eyes glared at Cycloid. Dressed in a pink shirt, pink shorts, and tall white boots, she didn't look like a typical Bakugan brawler. But Julie was as tough as the Subterra Bakugan she used in battle.

"What? How dare you! I'm not going anywhere,"

Julie shot back. She looked at Billy. "I can't believe you actually got a talking Bakugan. Where did you find him?"

Julie's friends Dan and Runo both had talking Bakugan, and now so did Billy. She wanted her own talking Bakugan more than anything — but she had no idea how to get one.

Billy ignored her question. "Yep, we're a perfect match," he said. He tipped the edge of his baseball cap with his finger. "I hate to say it, Julie, but you're toast!"

Julie's hands balled into fists. "That's it!" she exploded. "Let's brawl!"

Julie and Billy each held up a Bakugan Gate Card.

"Field Card Open!" they yelled at the same time.

The air around them shimmered as the Bakugan battlefield formed. The tumbleweeds stopped rolling as time within the field came to a standstill. Anyone who entered the valley now would not be able to enter or even see the field.

The two brawlers threw out their Gate Cards. Julie's landed in front of Billy, and Billy's landed in front of Julie. The two cards touched end-to-end to form one long rectangle.

Billy winked at Julie. "Okay, Baku-babe. Why don't you show me what you've got?"

Julie jumped up and down angrily. She was getting pretty tired of Billy's trash-talking. "What did you just call me?" she fumed.

She tossed a brown Bakugan ball onto the field. "Bakugan Brawl!"

The Bakugan landed on the card in front of Julie and popped open.

"Rattleoid Stand!" Julie yelled.

The Subterra Bakugan took its true form, and a giant snake appeared on the card, hissing at Billy. Its long, thick body had brown and yellow stripes. Sharp spikes stuck out of the rattle on the end of its tail. Two long, sharp fangs protruded from its mouth.

"Try *that* on for size!" Julie said smugly.

"Pretty impressive," Billy admitted. He pushed down the brim of his cap. "Bakugan Brawl!"

He threw out a brown Bakugan ball. It landed on the same card as Rattleoid. "Hynoid, Stand!"

The ball transformed into a Subterra Hynoid — a creature that looked like a werewolf.

"Do it!" Billy shouted.

Hynoid sprang across the card, its sharp claws outstretched. Julie knew that if Hynoid attacked Rattleoid now, her Bakugan would lose the round. Hynoid had 310 Gs, and Rattleoid had 300.

But Julie knew just what card to throw next.

"Ability Card Activate!" she cried. "Poison Fang!"

Rattleoid's eyes glowed with red fire.

"Hey, wait!" Billy protested.

But it was too late.

"Fifty Gs transferred from Hynoid to Rattleoid," reported Julie's Baku-pod, a small computer that kept track of the battle. Billy watched in dismay as Hynoid was left with 260 Gs, compared to Rattleoid's 350 points of G Power.

"Sorry, I know we've been friends a long time, Billy, but I need to teach you a lesson!" Julie called out.

Hynoid jumped back. If he attacked now, there was no way he could win. But Billy had some moves up his sleeve, too.

"Ha! That was just a warm up," he said. "Gate Card Open Now!"

Hynoid roared as a ring of fiery energy sprang up under his feet. A golden glow shone from his body.

"Hynoid's power level doubled to five-twenty Gs," the Baku-pod said.

Billy grinned. "Friend or no friend, you're going down!"

Julie frowned. "This doesn't look too good." 520 Gs was a lot of power!

"Go, Hynoid!" Billy commanded. "Take him out!"

Hynoid leaped up and grabbed Rattleoid by the throat with his powerful jaws. The ground shook as the big snake slammed onto the battlefield.

"Ha!" Billy cried triumphantly. "You sure showed *me* . . . nice one!"

Hynoid turned back into a ball and rolled to a stop at Billy's feet.

"Humph!" Julie said. "That was only *my* warm up, smart guy!"

Julie threw another Subterra Bakugan ball onto the field.

"Bakugan Brawl!"

The ball landed on the one Gate Card left on the field.

"Tuskor, Stand!"

The ball transformed into a massive mammoth with a long trunk and four sharp, curved tusks. Its coarse fur was brown and orange.

"Tuskor power level, three hundred fifty Gs," reported the Baku-pod.

"Ha," Billy said smugly. He threw Hynoid onto the field again. It landed on the same card as Tuskor. "Hynoid Stand!"

The werewolf-like creature appeared on the field once more and growled.

"And now, Ability Card Activate!" Billy shouted. "Whirlwind!"

Hynoid began to spin around and around like some kind of tornado. Tuskor shook its head from side to side and trumpeted loudly as the Bakugan came near.

Billy laughed. "Check that out! Your Tuskor doesn't know which way to turn."

Julie wasn't worried. On the field, Hynoid was spinning more and more slowly. He began to pant with exhaustion.

"Hynoid's power level . . . decreasing . . . decreasing . . . decreasing," her Baku-pod announced.

"Hynoid, what's the matter?" Billy asked, panicked. "What's going on?"

"Hynoid's power being decreased due to Poison Fang Ability Card still in effect," his Baku-pod calmly exclaimed.

Billy shook his head. "No way!"

"It'll continue to decrease as long as he keeps battling," Julie said confidently.

"Hynoid's power level still decreasing."

The Bakugan's power dropped all the way down to 260 Gs.

"Now, Tuskor!" Julie cried.

Billy gasped in shock as Tuskor stomped on Hynoid with one massive foot. Hynoid turned back into a Bakugan ball and bounced back to Billy. Julie had won the round.

"Now . . . Gate Card set!" Julie called out. She threw another card on the field. It landed in front of her. "Bakugan Brawl!"

Julie tossed Tuskor on the field again. Billy looked down at the new Bakugan ball in his hand.

"This is it," he said. "I'm depending on you, Cycloid."

Cycloid popped open. "No problemo, coach. Just put me in!"

Billy stepped forward and pulled back his arm like a baseball pitcher getting ready to throw a strike. "Bakugan Brawl! Cycloid Stand!"

Cycloid roared as he transformed into his true form. He looked like a giant on the field. A loincloth hung around his waist. Orange tribal markings decorated his chest. In his right hand he held a huge club.

"Cycloid's power is at three hundred seventy Gs," reported Julie's Baku-pod. That was 20 more than Tuskor's 350 Gs.

Julie wasn't worried. She was counting on the Gate Card she threw down to help her win the battle.

"Gate Card Open Now!" Julie cried. "Triple Battle! This card allows the battle to start when a third Bakugan is on the Field Card."

Julie got ready to throw another Bakugan onto the card. That would make it two Bakugan against one. She'd be sure to win the round.

But before she could make her move, Billy held up a card.

"No more Mr. Nice Guy. Ability Card Activate!" he shouted. "Smackdown!"

The card glowed brightly, and Cycloid's right hand became enormous. He brought it down on the Gate Card, smashing it into pieces.

"Oh no!" cried a horrified Julie. "My Gate Card!"

Now that she couldn't use Triple Battle, her Tuskor would be easy prey for Cycloid. Billy grinned.

"Give him a love tap, Cycloid," Billy commanded.

"Booyaaaa!" Cycloid cheered. He smacked Tuskor with his massive fist. Tuskor turned back into a ball and landed in Julie's hands.

Billy laughed. "That's how you brawl, Baku-babe."

Cycloid joined in. "Ya better go home. I think I hear your momma callin'."

But Julie was more determined to win than ever.

"I'm not going anywhere!" she said defiantly. She threw out a new Gate Card. "I'll show you. Bakugan Brawl! Manion Stand!"

A Subterra Manion appeared on the Gate Card. It looked like an ancient Egyptian sphinx, a creature with the body of a lion and the head of a man. Manion had clawed feet, a brown feathered lower body, and golden wings. Its lion's mane looked like a gold pharoah's headpiece.

Julie held up a card. "Ability Card Activate. Earth Power!"

"Manion's power level . . . three hundred and fifty Gs," her Baku-pod announced.

"Ooh, scary," Billy said calmly. "Bakugan Brawl! Cycloid Stand!"

Cycloid appeared on the field once more. "I'm baaaaaack!" he said. "And I'm feelin' nasty!"

Julie folded her arms in front of her. She was not going to let Cycloid win again. Her Gate Card would make sure of that.

"Gate Card, Open Now!" she called out. "Character!"

Before the card could turn over, Cycloid looked over his shoulder at Billy. "So, whaddya got for me?"

"This," Billy said. "Ability Card Activate!"

He held up a card. It was a duplicate of the last card he'd used. "Smackdown!"

Julie groaned. "Oh no. Not this again!"

"Okay, Cycloid, do your thing!" Billy commanded.

Cycloid raised his huge fist in the air. "Anybody need a *hand*?" he joked.

But Julie wasn't laughing. Cycloid destroyed the Gate Card, wiping out any chance Julie had to give Manion a boost of power. Cycloid turned to Manion next.

Bam!

"Manion defeated," said the Baku-pod.

"I don't believe it — he beat me!" Julie wailed. She hung her head. "I lost!"

The Bakugan field vanished around them. They were back in the dusty valley. Billy smiled at the brown Bakugan ball in his hand.

"All right, we did it, Cycloid!" he cheered. "You're the man."

"No, *you're* the man!" Cycloid replied.

Billy thrust the ball toward Julie. "Did you see how the two of us worked together?" he bragged. "The very moment I found him deep in the heart of Bakugan Valley, I *knew* we were meant to be together."

"In Bakugan Valley?" Julie asked. She looked around. If Billy had found a talking Bakugan here, there might be more of them.

"You betcha!" Billy answered. "In a remote corner . . . in the deepest cavern . . . there he was, just waiting for his destiny. And then we took you down!"

"You were lucky!" Julie shot back. "I don't need a 'perfect match' anyway. And next time I'll take the two of *you* down!"

Billy laughed. "Anytime, Baku-babe. Anytime."

Julie growled angrily through gritted teeth. Billy's smug attitude was too much.

"I can't stand him!" she fumed.

That night, Julie logged on to the computer in her bedroom. Her desk, chair, and even the computer were all pink, her favorite color.

Julie really needed to talk to somebody about her battle with Billy. Luckily, her four best Bakugan friends were online. Their faces popped on the screen for a webcam chat. Blue-haired Runo and Marucho, a boy with blond hair and glasses, were on the top of the screen. Alice and Dan's faces were on the bottom. Runo, Marucho, and Dan all had their talking Bakugan with them.

"I lost a Bakugan battle today to my childhood friend, Billy!" Julie wailed.

"Oh no," said Alice, a girl with kind brown eyes and red hair. "That's the real loudmouth guy, isn't it?"

Julie nodded. "Yeah."

"Oh man, that stinks!" said Dan. His Pyrus Bakugan, Drago, was perched on Dan's keyboard.

"Of course it does," Julie said. "Billy can be a real jerk sometimes, and it makes me wanna scream! To top it off, his Bakugan is just as bad."

Marucho's Aquos Bakugan, Preyas, spoke up. "Oh really? What is his Bakugan's name?"

"Um, I think it was Cycloid," Julie replied.

"Interesting," Preyas said. "Tigrerra, do you know this Cycloid?"

The talking Bakugan had all fallen through a hole between their dimension, Vestroia, and Earth. Many of them had known each other back in Vestroia.

"No, I don't know him," Tigrerra answered.

"How about you, Drago?" Dan asked.

"Yes," Drago replied. "A rather big fellow, as I recall."

"I'd sure like to throw down and see who's tougher, huh Drago?" Dan asked. He loved a challenge. "We could show them what a *real* team brawls like."

"Yeah, sounds great," Drago said. It was obvious to everyone but Dan that he didn't really mean it.

"I gotta say, Julie, you don't know what you're missing not having a Bakugan you can talk to," Dan said. He didn't realize he might be hurting Julie's feelings.

Marucho tried to make her feel better. "I'm sure you'll

meet one any time now and the two of you will get on famously!" he promised.

"I'm perfectly fine," Julie lied. "I'm happy just the way I am, thank you. I don't need a talking Bakugan to feel good about myself."

She pushed her chair back. "Well, good night everybody. Talk to ya later!"

She quickly shut off her computer. She didn't want to talk about talking Bakugan anymore. It just made her feel sad.

Julie changed into her pajamas and took her hair out of its ponytail. A full moon shone through her open window. She paused for a moment, gazing at the moon.

"The truth is . . . I'm not perfectly fine," she said with a sigh.

She fell back on her bed. Something caught her eye — a small toy on top of her bookshelf. It was a cowboy riding on a horse. A memory came flooding back to her.

She couldn't have been more than five years old. Billy had handed her the toy.

"Wow, thank you so much, Billy!" Julie had said. "You and me are gonna be best friends forever, I can just *feel* it!"

But Billy hadn't treated her like a best friend today. He had changed, and it all started when he found his talking Bakugan.

"*I* found him deep in the heart of Bakugan Valley," Billy had said.

Julie sat up.

"I do have a day off tomorrow," she said. "I suppose I could go to Bakugan valley . . ."

Deep down, Julie knew she might be going on a wild goose chase. Bakugan Valley was large, too big to explore in just one day. The rocky cliffs were filled with thousands of cracks and crevices where a Bakugan could be hiding. There were more caves than she could count.

But Julie wanted a talking Bakugan more than anything. The next morning, she headed to Bakugan Valley before the sun got too hot. She started to climb up one of the cliff sides.

"Like I said, I don't *need* a talking Bakugan to feel good about myself," she said as she reached up to grab another hold in the rock. "But everyone else seems to have one, and I think . . ."

Julie's sneaker slipped as she took her next step. With a cry, she tumbled backwards. She couldn't stop! She half-rolled, half-slid down the side of the cliff.

Then the ground opened up underneath her, and she realized she was falling through a hole. She landed with a thud on the floor of a dark cave.

"Ouch!" Julie cried.

The sound of her voice sent a swarm of bats flying at her. She screamed and fell to her knees to avoid them.

"Aaaaah!" Julie screamed again. The floor was crawling with scorpions!

Julie jumped to her feet and ran as fast as she could. The bats flew after her.

"Somebody get me out of here!" she cried out. "I don't need a talking Bakugan! Not if it means putting up with icky caves and icky bats and icky bugs and other icky stuff!"

CHAPTER 4

GOREM SPEAKS

Back home, Julie flopped on her bed. She felt defeated.

"I wasted my entire day off running around Bakugan Valley," she complained, "and I have absolutely nothing to show for it."

She sat up. "Oh well. I'm happy just the way I am. I'm fine battling without a companion," she said, trying to convince herself. "I don't need any talking Bakugan. I'm fine! Just because everybody else has one . . ."

Her mind drifted to the night before, when Dan bragged about using Drago to take down Billy.

We could show them what a real team brawls like!

Dan and Drago were a team. Julie knew she couldn't kid herself anymore. She wanted to be part of a team too.

"The truth is, I want to have a Bakugan to talk to

more than anything," she said, her voice breaking. "More than anything in the world!"

Julie began to sob. She had searched so hard. It just wasn't fair!

"Julie . . ."

Julie stopped crying when she heard her name. The voice was deep, but kind and gentle.

"I'm here."

Julie gasped. The voice was coming from her bookshelf. A brown Bakugan ball sat next to the toy Billy had given her when they were small.

"I'm here for *you*," the Bakugan told her.

"For me?" Julie was shocked. Was this some kind of dream?

"Like you, I have longed for a companion with whom to share my joys and sorrows," the Bakugan said. "I began to despair that it would ever come to be. But finally a pure and sincere voice reached me. Your voice!"

"I think I get it," Julie said. "Until now, I wasn't being honest with myself. My voice wasn't pure and honest enough to be heard by you. But you were there all along."

"Now that the barrier that separated us is gone, I feel as if I've known you for ages, though we've only just met," the Bakugan said.

Excited, Julie stood up. "Yes! It's like we're best friends

already," she said. "My name's Julie. May I ask what your name is?"

"I am Subterra Gorem," the Bakugan replied.

Julie repeated the name dreamily. "Subterra Gorem." Her very own talking Bakugan!

"You can just call me Gorem."

Julie picked up the Bakugan ball and held it close to her cheek. "Oh, Gorem. Let's be friends forever and ever and ever! Sound good?"

"Sounds good," Gorem answered.

Julie couldn't wait to use Gorem in battle. The next day, she met Billy in Bakugan Valley for another brawl. The two friends faced each other across the orange dusty ground.

"You're going down, Billy!" Julie cried out confidently.

"You gonna teach me another lesson today?" Billy scoffed. "You're the one who never learns!"

Julie was ready for Billy's big mouth. She wasn't going to let it get to her this time.

"I have finally found my Baku-partner!" Julie said defiantly.

"Oh good! You've finally managed to find yourself a talking Bakugan," Billy said. He sounded happy for his friend. "Well in that case . . . it's time to battle!"

"All right!" Julie agreed. "It's showtime!"

Each player held up a Gate Card. "Field Open!" Once again, time came to a stop outside the field of play.

"Gate Card Set!" They tossed out the cards, which landed on the ground end to end to form the field.

"Okay, Julie," Billy said. "Time for the second inning."

He pitched a brown Bakugan ball onto the field. "Bakugan Brawl! Hynoid Stand!"

Hynoid landed on the card directly in front of Julie and growled. He was ready to brawl.

"My turn!" Julie said. She threw another Gate Card onto the field. The card landed to the right of the card Hynoid was standing on.

Julie tossed out a Bakugan ball next. "Bakugan Brawl!"

The ball landed on the new Gate Card. "Tuskor, Stand!"

"Tuskor's power level: three hundred and fifty Gs," announced the Baku-pod.

Julie wasn't done yet. She held up a card. "Ability Card Activate! Nose Slap!"

Tuskor's long trunk grew even longer.

"With this, he can reach out and attack the Bakugan

standing on the next card," Julie explained. "All right, Tuskor, take him out!"

Tuskor stomped loudly with his front legs and then roared. He swung his long trunk at Hynoid and hit the Bakugan with a loud slap.

Billy shook his head in disbelief as Hynoid's Bakugan ball landed at his feet. The Gate Card disappeared and landed on Julie's side of the field.

"Pretty good, Julie," he admitted. "But not good enough!"

Billy threw out a new Gate Card that landed end-to-end with Tuskor's card. Then he wound up like a baseball pitcher and tossed another Bakugan ball on the field.

"Bakugan Brawl!" The ball landed on the new Gate Card. "Wormquake Stand!"

A giant brown wormlike monster appeared on the card. Subterra Wormquake had no face, just a wide, gaping mouth filled with sharp teeth.

"Wormquake power level: three hundred and forty Gs," reported the Baku-pod.

Billy held up a card. "Ability Card Activate. Sandtrap!"

Wormquake's Gate Card began to shake. The giant worm dove under the card as though it were sand. Then it burst through the Gate Card Tuskor was standing on. The big Bakugan trumpeted in fear.

Julie wasn't worried. "Come on, Tuskor's power level is three hundred fifty Gs. You won't beat him with a lame attack like that!"

Billy grinned. "Here's a little tidbit for ya. You see, the cool thing about Sandtrap is that it knocks down the opponent's power level . . . check it!"

"Tuskor's power level is decreased by fifty Gs."

Julie gasped as Tuskor's power level dropped down to 300 Gs. "Now Wormquake is stronger!"

Tuskor's Bakugan ball bounced and landed at her feet. Panicked, she took Gorem's Bakugan ball from her pack and held it up to her face.

"Please help me, Gorem!" she pleaded. "I think I'm in real trouble here. I need you. Help me!"

"Don't worry," Gorem assured her. "I will do my very best to help you."

"So then, where's this new Bakugan you were so proud of?" Billy called from across the field.

Julie hurled Gorem's Bakugan ball onto the field. "Okay, Gorem, show me your stuff!"

The ball landed on the card with Wormquake. "Gorem, Stand!"

But Gorem did not transform into his true form. Instead, the Bakugan ball bounced back to Julie.

"Gorem?" Julie asked. She picked him up. "Oh no, Gorem, what's the matter? Did I do something wrong?"

"The time isn't right," Gorem said.

"Not right? What are you talking about?" Julie asked, her voice rising.

"Trust me," Gorem said calmly.

Julie wasn't sure what to think. "Oh no!" she wailed. "Then what on earth am I gonna do?"

CHAPTER 5

GOREM STAND!

illy laughed. "Looks like it's my turn," he said. "Gate Card Set!"

He threw out a new card. It landed in front of Julie.

"Okay, batter up!" he cried. "Bakugan Brawl!"

The brown Bakugan ball he tossed out landed on the new Gate Card. "Cycloid Stand!"

Billy's one-eyed powerhouse appeared on the field, holding a heavy club in one hand.

"Ability Card Activate!" Billy cried, holding up a card. "Stare Down!"

Cycloid's large eye began to glow. A red-hot laser beam shot out, and Cycloid used the beam to draw a rectangular line around the field.

"You're in for it now," Billy bragged. "With this ability, my Bakugan can decrease the power level of every Bakugan on every card within the red border by fifty Gs."

"Then I'll add a card outside of it," Julie said, her blue eyes gleaming. "How do you like that?"

She positioned her Gate Card just outside of the red border. Then she tossed out a Bakugan ball. "Bakugan Brawl!"

The ball landed on the card she had just added. "Manion Stand!"

Subterra Manion appeared, gently flapping its huge wings.

Julie held up a card. "Ability Card Activate! Copycat!"

Billy frowned, worried. "Copycat? Then that means you can . . ."

"That's right," Julie said smugly. "I can copy Wormquake's ability, Sandtrap, and use it against him!"

Now Manion could attack Sandtrap from the safety of his own Gate Card. Wormquake shrieked and collapsed on the field. Julie had won the round — and now Billy was down two Bakugan. Cycloid was his only chance to win.

"Pretty good," Billy grudgingly admitted. "Now try *this* on for size. Ability Card Activate! Grand Slide!"

Julie gasped as Manion's Gate Card was pulled into the rectangle, right next to Cycloid's Gate Card!

"Manion moved within Stare Down perimeter," the Baku-pod reported. *"Manion power level decreased by fifty Gs."*

"Oh, nooo!" Julie wailed. There was nothing she could to do help Cycloid now.

"Get ready, cause this just might hurt," Cycloid warned Manion. Then . . . BAM! He brought down his club on Julie's Bakugan.

Manion's Bakugan ball rolled back to Julie, "No, Manion!" she cried.

"Okay, I've waited long enough, Julie," Billy said. "Time to meet this new Bakugan of yours."

"I want a new playmate!" Cycloid chimed in.

"What should I do?" Julie wondered out loud. "Gorem said to trust him and wait!" But Tuskor and Manion were out of the game — she could only use one more Bakugan. She held Gorem's Bakugan ball in the palms of her hands, hesitant.

"Julie, I cannot bear to see you tormented like this," Gorem said gently. "I told you I wanted to share your joys and sorrows."

Julie hesitated. "Gorem . . ."

"Julie, throw me in," Gorem said.

"What?" Julie asked. "But I can't risk losing my perfect match."

"Trust me," Gorem said. His voice was soothing and calm. "The time is now. Don't worry. Now that I've found you, I won't abandon you."

Julie was moved. She had only just met Gorem, yet he cared for her so much. "Thank you so much, Gorem," she told her new friend. "Thank you for finding me. I promise that I won't let you down either."

"Come on!" Billy called out impatiently.

"Okay, here goes," Julie said. She held Gorem's Bakugan ball high above her head, then leaned back dramatically. She sprang back up, tossing out the ball at the same time. "Bakugan Brawl! Heads up!"

Gorem's Bakugan ball smacked Cycloid in the head and landed on the card in front of him. Cycloid got knocked right on his butt.

"Gorem Stand!" Julie shouted.

A low, thunderous growl rose up as Gorem transformed into his true form. The gigantic Subterra Bakugan towered over the field like a skyscraper. Gorem's powerful body was protected by thick, stone armor. Red eyes glowed from under a black helmet that covered his head and face. He held a big, round shield in his left hand.

"Wh-what is that?" Billy asked nervously.

Julie couldn't believe her eyes. Gorem was even more awesome than she had imagined.

"That is Gorem!" she said proudly.

ven tough guy Cycloid looked scared. "He's gigantic!"

Gorem reached down and held open his palms. Julie stepped into his hands, and he gently lifted her up to his face.

"Oh, Gorem!" Julie said. "You're incredible! You are the best Bakugan a girl could hope for."

"I don't know," Cycloid said, trying to sound brave. "He doesn't look so tough. I'll have him saying 'uncle' in no time."

Julie stepped onto Gorem's shoulder and looked down at the field.

"Well, Cycloid, let's see if you're right," she said. She held up a card. "Ability Card Activate! Mega Impact!"

Gorem let out a loud roar. His body glowed red with extra energy.

"What's going on?" Billy asked.

"Gorem's power level increased by fifty Gs," the Baku-pod said. Julie smiled happily as she watched her Bakugan's power grow.

"For hundred and thirty Gs?" Billy asked in disbelief. "No messing around, Cycloid. We gotta take this guy out fast!"

"I hear ya big time on that," Cycloid agreed.

Billy had one move left, and he hoped it would be enough to win.

"Gate Card open!" he cried. The card the Bakugan were standing on flipped over.

"The Level Down Command Card decreases power by one hundred Gs," Billy announced.

Gorem roared as his power level dropped.

"Gorem's power level reduced to three hundred and thirty Gs."

"Okay, Cycloid, now's your chance!" Billy commanded fiercely.

Cycloid grunted and charged across the field. "The bigger they are the harder they fall!"

"Gorem!" Julie cried in alarm.

"It's Hammer Time!" Cycloid shouted as he brought down his huge club.

Bam! The club hit Gorem's shield.

Bam! Cycloid tried again, but Gorem's shield absorbed the blow again.

Bam! Bam! Cycloid didn't want to give up. He kept pounding away.

"This is bad," Billy realized. "That shield is too strong and Cycloid's power level goes down with every blow!"

Cycloid stopped, panting with exhaustion. "Uh oh."

"Cycloid's power level reduced to two hundred and seventy Gs."

Angry, Cycloid delivered one last, massive blow.

BAM!

His hammer shattered into pieces.

"What?" Billy asked in surprise.

"This is it, Gorem!" Julie said.

Gorem pulled back his right arm and smacked Cycloid with a big punch. Cycloid turned back into a Bakugan ball and rolled back to Billy.

Julie jumped up and down, excited. "Gorem, you big beautiful Bakugan, you did it! You did it! You did it! Yes! Yes! Yes!"

Then the Bakugan field vanished. Julie and Billy were back in Bakugan Valley.

Billy walked up to her. Julie hoped they could still be friends.

"Billy?" she asked.

She didn't have to worry. Billy gave her a big smile and handed her back Gorem's Bakugan ball.

"Good job, Julie. You two battle well together," he said.

"Thank you," Julie replied. "I think Gorem and I are a perfect match for each other!"

Billy held Cycloid in his hand. "Good job out there, Gorem," Cycloid said sincerely.

"You too, Cycloid," Gorem said.

Billy held Cycloid up to his face. "Okay, Cycloid, come on," he said. "We need to start training! I think we're getting soft."

"We can't have that now, can we?" Cycloid agreed. "Gotta keep in tip top brawlin' shape!"

"Yeah," Billy said. "See ya, Julie!"

Julie waved as Billy walked away. "See ya Billy! I can't wait till we get to battle each other again!"

Julie raced home. She couldn't wait to tell her friends what had happened. That night, she talked to them all via webcam on her computer.

Gorem's Bakugan ball popped open. She held him up to the camera.

"I'd like to introduce you to my new special friend. His name is Gorem," Julie told everyone.

"Wow, Julie!" Dan said. "You finally found a talking Bakugan?"

"You bet I did!" Julie said proudly.

"Aw, that's great," Marucho said. "I'm so happy for you."

Marucho's Preyas jumped up in front of him. "Hi there, Mr. Gorem. I'm so pleased to meet you. I'm Preyas, and this is Drago."

"Drag what?" Gorem asked.

"Drag-o," Dan's Drago said.

"My Bakugan is called Tig," Runo said happily. She held up her Haos Tigrerra. "Say hello, Tig."

"Tig?" Gorem asked, confused. That didn't sound like a Bakugan name.

"Call me Tigrerra," Tigrerra said, correcting Runo.

"Gorem, you have lots of friends now. Isn't that great?" Julie asked. She cupped Gorem in her hands and held him up to her face.

"Looks like you two are best friends," Alice remarked.

"You bet!" Julie replied. "Gorem and I are the best-est friends in the whole wide world. Isn't that right, Gorem?"

She gave a quick little kiss to Gorem's Bakugan ball.

"Not in front of people," Gorem said shyly.

Julie and her friends laughed.

"Welcome aboard, Gorem!" Tigrerra said.

CHAPTER 7

BATTLE ON THE PIER

Julie's friends Dan, Runo, and Marucho all lived in the same city. They often got together just to hang out. Lately, though, things had become much more serious.

A mysterious brawler named Masquerade had appeared on the scene a few weeks before. Masquerade used a special card called the Doom Card. When he defeated his opponents, their Bakugan were sent into the terrible Doom Dimension.

For some reason, Masquerade was targeting Dan and his friends. He kept sending other brawlers after them to do his dirty work. Lately, it seemed like one of Masquerade's brawlers challenged them every time they turned around.

Today was no different. Dan, Runo, and Marucho

were hanging out by the river when a punked-out looking kid approached them on the pier. He had spiky, light blue hair with a purple streak going through it. His eyes were light blue, and he wore a pale blue shirt. He immediately challenged them to a brawl.

"So, ya chicken?" he asked. He held out his right arm to show off his round, blue Bakugan shooter.

Dan sighed. "Another lackey of Masquerade's?"

"Yeah, this is starting to get old," Runo agreed. Then she cheered up. "But just for fun, let me show him who's boss!"

"No way, I call dibs on this creep!" Dan said. He started to walk down the pier.

"Hey, no fair!" Runo complained.

Marucho looked worried. "Dan, wait!"

Dan and the blue-haired brawler faced off. They each held up a Gate Card.

"Field Open!"

Runo and Marucho froze, stopped in time, as the field formed around Dan and his opponent. The battle was fierce from the start. The punk kid used Ventus Bakugan, and his strategy was pretty good. In the end, the kid's Ventus Gargonoid faced off against Dan's Pyrus Drago.

Gargonoid looked like a living, breathing gargoyle statue. Two long horns grew on top of its monstrous head. Two huge, green wings grew from its back. Drago looked like a huge, red dragon with gold scales down its belly and big, gold wings.

Gargonoid furiously flapped its wings, causing a tornadolike wind to whip up. Drago gave a ferocious roar as the wind tore through him.

"Come on, Drago, defense!" Dan called out.

The tornado wind raced across the field, aimed for Drago.

"Must . . . resist . . ." Drago said through gritted teeth.

He braced himself for the impact. If he could withstand this attack, Dan would win the battle.

"Drago, hold on!" Dan urged.

Drago stood firm — but the winds slammed into Dan. As the battle ended, the Bakugan field disappeared. Dan was hurled backward onto the pier right in front of Runo and Marucho.

Time started again, and Runo picked up talking where she had left off.

"No fair! You're butting in, Dan!" Then she noticed Dan sprawled at her feet. "Huh?"

The punk kid jumped into a speedboat tied to the pier.

"You just got lucky, that's all!" he called out, untying his boat. "I'll be back, ya freaks!"

The boy sped off. Runo looked after him in disbelief.

"So I'm guessing you beat him?" Runo asked.

"Way to go, Dan!" Marucho said proudly. He was a few years younger than Dan and Runo, and a lot shorter. "I had total confidence you could do it!"

"Ah, it was nothing," Dan bragged. He suddenly felt strangely light-headed. "I had him . . . on . . . the ropes . . ."

Dan fell over and hit the pier with a thud. Runo and Dan gasped and knelt by him. His eyes were closed, and he wasn't moving.

"Dan, no!" Marucho yelled. "Are you okay? Dan! Can you hear me? Wake up!"

Dan woke up later in a comfortable bed in one of the many rooms in the giant mansion where Marucho lived. He moaned weakly as he opened his eyes. Marucho sat in a chair on one side of the bed, and Runo stood on the other.

"Man, that was way out there on the freaky scale," Dan said. "I remember I beat the dude, but after that, it's a total blank."

"Oh, that was so hilarious Dan," Marucho said, trying to make his friend feel better. "The way that wannabe brawler ran away with his tail between his legs."

"Well, it's kind of your own fault, Mr. Buttinski!" Runo snapped. She was still upset that Dan had started the battle before she had a chance to brawl.

Dan sat up. "I knew this was going to be a snooze fest!" he complained. "I'm just lucky that Drago was tough enough to take that chump out when he did."

"According to my data, we will face much stronger opponents," Marucho warned. The young boy was a walking Bakugan encyclopedia. He knew every rule of the game inside and out. "I might suggest our strategy should reflect this in any future battles."

"In English," Runo said calmly. Sometimes Marucho talked like an encyclopedia, too.

"Meaning a Bakugan is at its peak when all of its six attributes are in perfect alignment," Marucho explained. "Dan's Bakugan is Drago and it's a Pyrus, a Fire Attribute. Yours is a Haos, a Light Attribute. And my Preyas is classified as an Aquos — that's Water. But the problem is, combined, we don't have enough attributes to fight at full power."

"Add on Julie's, which is Subterra, the Earth Attribute," Dan reminded him.

"That means we're two short," Runo added. "Darkus, with its Darkness Attribute, and the Wind Attribute, Ventus."

"Hey, guess who has Ventus?" Marucho asked, excited.

"Shun!" Dan blurted out. He folded his arms across his chest. Dan did not look happy. He and Shun used to be friends. Then Shun became the number-one ranked Bakugan brawler, and everything had changed.

"Correct, Dan," Marucho said. "Right now, Masquerade is stronger than us. I suggest we align ourselves to Shun to increase our power and defeat Masquerade."

"Brilliant!" Runo agreed. "With Shun on our team, we'll be a force to be reckoned with. No one will even come close to beating us. Not to mention Shun's a real hunk. Right, Dan?"

Dan fumed silently. He really didn't feel like hearing about how great Shun was.

But Marucho was really pleased. "This is the most

impeccable proposal I believe we have ever engineered," he said eagerly. "What do you think, Dan?"

"No!" Dan replied.

"But Dan, we need all the help we can get," Runo pointed out. "Or maybe you're just jealous."

"I am not!" Dan said. "Besides, I don't need any help. From him or anybody else, including you, Runo. You got that?"

Dan flopped back down and pulled the covers over his head.

"Yep, you're jealous," Runo said with a teasing smile.

Dan rolled over with his back to Runo.

"Girls!" he muttered. "Who needs 'em?"

CHAPTER 8

THE SEARCH FOR SHUN

That night, Marucho and Runo snuck away while Dan was sleeping. They boarded the private plane owned by Marucho's family. The small plane was piloted by the family butler, a quiet man with a bald head and gray mustache. The plane took off from the roof of the skyscraper-like mansion and soared into the starry sky.

"Boy, if Dan finds out what we're doing, he's going to be sooo mad!" Marucho said, worried.

"Relax, Marucho," Runo said calmly. "We have to ask Shun to help us. And trust me, Dan will thank us!"

Marucho gazed out the window. "I hope so."

"I wonder why Dan is so dead set against Shun?" Runo asked. "I remember they used to be the best of buds. They were even the ones who came up with all of the Bakugan rules."

"Wow, that's almost interesting!" Marucho's Preyas said sarcastically. The Bakugan was perched on Marucho's palm.

"Call me crazy, but I thought for sure that Dan would want to hook up with Shun again," Runo said. She just couldn't figure it out.

Marucho pointed out the window. "Look, Runo. I believe that's Shun's house down there."

Runo gazed past him. The plane had flown out of the downtown area. Below them was a sprawling house surrounded by trees.

Runo was surprised. "What?" It was the biggest home she'd ever seen, next to Marucho's mansion.

"According to my research, the Shun family owns the largest estate west of Bay City," Marucho explained.

The plane landed on Shun's front lawn. Runo and Marucho walked up to the large wood front gate.

Runo was impressed. "Big bucks *and* good looks! Hello, Shun!"

"Ah, Runo, we're here on business," Marucho reminded her. "Besides, what if Shun decides he's not interested in joining us? Our whole mission would be a failure. And worse, we could lose our Bakugan!"

"Quit being such a worrywart," Runo scolded. "Now let's get this over with! Hey Shun!"

The gates immediately swung open.

"That was fast," Runo remarked.

They stepped through the gates onto a smooth white walkway. It led to the front house, a traditional Japanese-style building. They slid open the doors, which were made of bamboo posts and lined with rice paper.

The room they entered was long and narrow, with gleaming wood floors. It was completely bare of furniture.

"I wouldn't want to be the one who has to vacuum this place," Runo joked as they stepped inside.

"You think anyone's home?" Marucho asked nervously.

"No clue," Runo replied. "But let's keep looking."

Their footsteps echoed as they walked down the long room. "This place reminds me of your house, Marucho," Runo said. "One big, over-sized mansion without enough bathrooms."

Then Runo felt something hit her ankle. She had walked into some kind of wire. The wire stretched out of the room and hung outside. Slats of wood dangled from the wire, and they rattled together when Runo hit it. She had triggered some kind of alarm.

"Uh-oh. What did I do?" Runo wondered.

Before she could react, a panel slid down on the walls on either side of them. Wood poles shot out of holes in the panels, attacking them from either side.

"Let's get out of here!" Runo cried.

They raced ahead. More panels slid down, and more poles shot out. They managed to dodge them all except the last one, which hit them in the knees. Runo and Marucho both tumbled forward.

They quickly got up and raced on. Up ahead, the floor opened to reveal a trap door. They screamed and jumped over it just in time. They fell to their knees when they reached the other side. Before they could get up, a net fell from the ceiling, trapping them.

"Aaaaaaaaaah!" they both screamed.

"This house is one big booby trap," Marucho remarked.

"You can say that again!" agreed Runo.

They struggled to get the net off. Then a cackling laugh filled the room.

"Well, what have we here? A couple of snoopy little kids who have the gall to break into my house!"

An old man stepped into the room. He had white hair and a thick, curly mustache. He wore puffy, knee-length pants, a tan shirt, and a green jacket. Rimless spectacles sat on the bridge of his nose.

"If you two little whippersnappers think you're smarter than me, then you have got another thing coming!"

Runo leaned over to Marucho. "You got any clue on the old dude in the sweatpants?" she whispered.

"That's Shun's grandfather," Marucho whispered back. "He used to be a famous ninja warrior back when there used to be ninja warriors."

"You're kidding!" Runo blurted out.

"State your business here," Grandpa Shun said barked grumpily. "Or prepare to face my . . . wooden stick!"

Grandpa Shun took a wooden stick from behind his back and brandished it in front of him.

"Please put down the stick!" Marucho cried out. "We come in peace!"

"Yeah, we're friends of your grandson Shun," Runo explained. "W-we just want to see him."

"My grandson?" Grandpa Shun asked. He sounded suspicious. "You say you're friends?"

Runo smiled nervously. "My name is Runo and this is Marucho."

She quickly reached into Marucho's back pocket. "Hey, what are you doing?" Marucho protested. "Trying to give me a wedgie or something?"

Runo retrieved Preyas's blue Bakugan ball and held it out to Grandpa Shun. "See?" she said. "Show this to Shun and he'll explain everything to you."

"No! Please! Why me?" Preyas begged. His Bakugan ball popped open. "What did I do to you?"

He popped back into his ball. Runo tossed Preyas to Grandpa Shun. The ball bounced off his head and landed in his palm.

"Oh yes," Grandpa Shun said. "You're what they call Bakugan brawlers. I know all about you. And you're here to get Shun to play this silly game again?"

"Well, yeah, that's kinda what we were thinking," Runo said hopefully.

"That's what I thought!" Grandpa Shun snapped. "He's not interested. Now leave the premises at once, intruders!"

Runo pressed her palms together and gave him her best cute expression. "Please, please, please!" she begged. "Can't we just see him for five minutes? Please!"

"You're starting to get on my nerves, kid!" the old man replied. "Now beat it!"

"This isn't working," Runo whispered to Marucho. "But I've got an idea."

She stood up, throwing off the net. "Okay, grandpa, if you refuse to bring Shun to us, we'll just go find him ourselves!"

Marucho popped up. "Yeah," he said, trying to sound brave. "And just one thing. You mind giving me back my Bakugan?"

"Sure, what do I care?" Grandpa Shun said.

Preyas started to panic. "Not again!"

Grandpa Shun tossed Preyas into the air. Marucho caught it. Then the old man tossed something else — a smoke bomb! Smelly smoke filled the air. Marucho and Runo fell to their knees, coughing.

"Didn't you hear me?" Grandpa Shun yelled. "Leave!"

He lunged at them, his wooden stick raised in the air. Runo and Marucho screamed and closed their eyes. They moved to protect themselves with the only thing they had on hand. Without thinking, they each held a Gate Card in front of their face.

All around them, time stopped. Grandpa Shun was frozen, brandishing his wooden stick. The air around Runo and Marucho swirled with orange and yellow light. Preyas and Tigrerra were suspended in midair. The two friends stood up and looked around in wonder.

"Where are we?" Preyas asked groggily.

"A battlefield," Tigrerra replied.

"I accidentally threw down my Gate Card," Runo realized. "So, do you guys want to battle?"

"Are you nuts!" Preyas shrieked in horror.

"Wait a minute, I've got an idea," Marucho interrupted. "We stopped time when Shun's Grandpa was about to attack. All we have to do is find the exact spot where we were standing . . ."

"I think I catch your drift," Runo said. "Yeah, let's do it!"

Marucho studied the room. He took a few steps

to the side. "I do believe we were standing right about here."

"Okay, so we'll move over here," Runo said, pointing.

They moved a few feet away.

"Are you ready?" Marucho asked.

Runo nodded. They both shouted at once. "Field Card Close!"

Time started up again. Grandpa Shun lunged through the air once more. But Runo and Marucho had moved. He landed with a hard thud on the wood floor.

"This is going to leave a mark!" he cried.

He bounced up, somersaulted, and fell right through his own trap — the hole in the floor. He landed on his back, groaning. Runo and Marucho looked down at him with concern.

"Oh honey bun. Did you put the cat out?" he asked groggily.

Runo couldn't help giggling. Then she and Marucho heard a noise — the sound of a flute. The music was coming from outside.

"Shun!" Runo cried.

Runo and Marucho raced back outside. Shun was perched on the slanted rooftop of the house, playing a small round flute. His long, black hair was tied at the nape of his neck. He wore a purple short-sleeved shirt over a blue tank top. He had a brown band on each wrist.

"Hey, Shun!" Marucho called up.

Shun stopped playing and looked at them. His wide eyes were a pale shade of brown.

"We found you! I was beginning to get a little worried back there," Runo said.

"It's nice to see you again!" Marucho said happily.

Shun did not return his smile. "Why did you come here?"

"We know it's short notice, Shun, but we kind of need your help," Marucho explained.

"I don't know if you know this, but there's this really freaky dude who calls himself Masquerade and he's been sending kids' Bakugan to the Doom Dimension forever!" Runo chimed in.

"Yeah, and we have to stop him!" Marucho added. "He's challenged us to a battle and, before we agree, we need you and your Bakugan to boost our power. Without you, we could lose our Bakugan!"

Runo smiled. "So what do you say, Shun, you in or out? Well?"

Shun gazed up at the starry sky. He didn't answer.

"Well?" Runo asked again.

"Sorry," Shun replied coolly. "I don't play on a team."

Runo and Marucho were shocked.

Shun gave them a firm, cold stare. "Now leave!"

CHAPTER 10

SHUN'S CHALLENGE

The big wooden gates closed in front of Marucho and Runo.

"Now what?" Marucho wondered. They really needed Shun to join their team. He didn't want to give up now.

Runo knocked on the gate. "Shun, open up!"

Grandpa Shun popped out from behind a bush. "Didn't I tell you? My grandson doesn't want anything to do with you two. Now skedaddle, before I get all ninja on you!" He cackled gleefully.

Runo ignored him. She pounded on the gate. "Come on, Shun, let us in! Open the door!"

"Please, Shun, open up!" Marucho urged. "If you don't, then all the Bakugan rules that you and Dan created will be destroyed forever. You gotta let us in!"

"At least let us take you on in a battle," Runo pleaded. She raised her voice. "SHUN!"

Runo's voice carried across the estate to a small stone house. Inside, Shun sat on a loft platform with his back to the window. The loft was nearly bare, with only a bed and a chest of drawers. Moonlight streaming through the window was the only light in the room.

A calm female voice spoke to him from the shadows.

"Are you sure you want them to leave, Shun? If they do, I don't think they'll ever come back again. They came a long way just to talk to you."

"Yeah," Shun said.

A shaft of light illuminated the source of the voice: a pale green Bakugan ball.

"Oh, Shun . . ." the Bakugan said sadly.

"It's okay, Skyress," Shun said.

"If you're worried about me, don't," Skyress said. "Everything will be fine. You must stop running away from what's in your heart. After all, there will come a day when you will have to face up to it."

Skyress's ball popped open. She had the face of a bird and two green wings.

"And this just may be that time," she told him.

Shun walked across the room to the chest of drawers

and opened up the top one. Inside were two more green Bakugan balls and a deck of cards.

Runo and Marucho marched back to the plane. Tall pine trees grew on either side of the wide lawn.

"Boy, I can't believe what happened back there," Runo complained.

"I know," Marucho agreed. "First Dan blows us off. And then Shun doesn't want anything to do with us."

"If there's one thing I'll never figure, it's boys!" Runo said.

They could now see the hulking figure of the plane in front of them in the darkness. Marucho stopped. "Hey, Runo, think we should go back and try again?"

Suddenly, the front lights of the plane turned on. They shone right on Shun, who stood in front of the plane with his back to them.

"S-Shun . . ." Runo said in disbelief.

"Did you change your mind and decide to join up with us?" Marucho asked.

Shun turned to them, a thin smile on his face. "But only if you defeat me."

Runo grinned. "Sounds like a blast! I'm up for it!"

"No, let me, Runo," Marucho said eagerly. "I have a better chance, pitting my Aquos against his Ventus. You gotta trust me on this one."

"I'm ready when you're ready," Shun said calmly. "I'll take you both on."

"You can't be serious?" Runo asked.

Shun held up a Gate Card to show that he was. Runo and Marucho quickly did the same.

"Field Open!" all three brawlers yelled at once.

Time stopped around them as the field formed, a rectangle of plain white light surrounded by swirling light in a rainbow of colors. Runo looked at Shun across from them and shook her head.

"He doesn't know what he's doing. He's crazy!" she told Marucho. "Two against one! He doesn't stand a chance."

CHAPTER 11

WINDS OF FURY!

G ate Card set!" yelled the three brawlers.

They each threw a Gate Card onto the field. The three cards formed an L-shape.

"Okay, I'll go first!" Marucho said. "Bakugan Brawl!"

He tossed a blue Bakugan ball onto the field. It landed on one of the cards in front of Shun. "Terrorclaw Stand!"

The ball opened up, and Terrorclaw appeared in a blaze of blue light. The Aquos Bakugan looked like a giant crab, with a wide, flat head and huge, sharp pincers. A hard blue shell covered its body.

Shun threw next. His pale green Bakugan ball landed on the same card as Terrorclaw.

"Falconeer Stand!" Shun called out.

A half-human, half-hawk Bakugan burst from the ball. Palegreen Falconeer had a sharp beak and powerful wings. Plates of armor with gold markings protected his arms, legs, and chest. He flew straight up in the air and gave a loud battle screetch.

"Okay, Bakugan Gate Card Open!" Marucho cried. The card underneath the two Bakugan flipped over, and a big wave of water rose up behind Terrorclaw. The card gave his Aquos Bakugan an extra boost of power.

But Shun's turn wasn't over yet. He held up a card as purple and blue light shimmered behind him.

"All right! Ability Activate! Tornado Pandemonium!"

A twirling tornado appeared and raced across the field. It slammed into Terrorclaw's wave, and the water scattered everywhere. Marucho's Bakugan lost his extra protection.

Then Falconeer swooped in to attack.

Wham! He knocked down Terrorclaw, and the Bakugan transformed into a ball.

The round was over. Shun and Falconeer had won.

"Impossible!" Marucho cried.

"This isn't over yet," Runo promised. She added a new card to the field. It landed right in front of her. Then she threw out a white Bakugan ball.

The ball landed on the new card and transformed

into Ventus Saurus. The tough-looking Bakugan looked like a dinosaur on two legs. Gleaming gold and silver armor protected his white body. Two white horns protruded from under his helmet.

"*Saurus, two hundred and ninety Gs,*" her Baku-pod reported.

"But that's not enough Gs!" Marucho warned.

Runo smiled. "And that's exactly what he's thinking!" she said. "All I have to do is throw down my Saurus character card and double my power."

Shun made his move next. He put a new card on the field. This one touched Saurus' card. Now there were four cards down, forming a square.

He tossed out Falconeer again.

"*Falconeer . . . three hundred and twenty Gs.*"

Runo frowned, confused. "He didn't attack us!"

Shun didn't seem to be falling for her trap. "We've got to be careful and come up with a plan, Marucho," she said. She thought for a moment. "I got it!"

She whispered in Marucho's ear. He grinned.

"You know, crazy as it sounds, it just might work!"

Marucho held up a blue Bakugan ball. "Okay, Limulus, game on! Bakugan Brawl!"

He tossed the ball onto the field. It landed on the card next to Falconeer's card. "Limulus Stand!"

A big Bakugan that looked like a horseshoe crab appeared on the card. Claws wiggled underneath a round, hard blue shell. Two long appendages that looked like tentacles extended from under the front of its head.

"Limulus has entered the battle. No other data available," said the Baku-pod.

"We're looking good, Marucho!" Runo said. "Now time for phase two."

"You got it," Marucho promised. "Ability Card Activate! Holograph Divide!"

A round wave of rippling blue light bathed Limulus.

"With this defense shield, Limulus's power will increase as the battle intensifies," Marucho said proudly. "That's because he'll absorb the power used against him."

"And that makes our plan virtually unbeatable!" Runo said. "This is so cool!"

"Oh yeah?" Shun said defiantly. He tossed another Bakugan ball onto the field. It landed on the card next to Saurus. Now all four cards had Bakugan on them.

The ball burst open, and another Falconeer flew out.

"Falconeer Two has now entered battle," announced the Baku-pod.

"Didn't see that coming!" Marucho said, worried.

Runo sighed. They kept trying to bait Shun to battle them, but he wouldn't do it. "Back to the drawing board."

Tigrerra's Bakugan ball popped open in Runo's hand. "Well, looks like my turn," she said.

"What are you saying, Tigrerra?" Runo asked.

"Shun's Bakugan are on the verge of attacking. I know their moves," she explained. "Trust me."

Runo liked the sound of that. Tigrerra was her most powerful Bakugan.

Preyas flew up next to her. "Atta girl, Tigrerra! You get in there and show them who's boss!" he cheered.

Runo nodded. "This just might work! Let's do it!" She held up a new Gate Card.

"Okay, Tigrerra. We're all counting on you. Gate Card Set!" She threw a new Gate Card onto the field. It touched Saurus's card on the right.

"Introducing new player," announced the Baku-pod.

"Bakugan Brawl! Tigrerra Stand!" Runo yelled.

Haos Tigrerra bounced onto the new card and emerged from her ball in a blaze of white light. She looked like a powerful white tiger with massive jaws and muscular arms and legs. Tigrerra reared back her head and roared.

Shun held up his last Bakugan ball. "If I need you, are you there, Skyress?" he asked softly.

"Yes," his Bakugan replied.

"This is it!" Shun called out. "Bakugan Brawl!"

He tossed the ball onto the card with Tigrerra.

"Skyress Stand!"

The ball opened up, and a mass of black stormclouds appeared above the card. Lightning flashed as a blast of green energy shot up from the Bakugan ball and vanished inside the clouds. Then pale light glowed from the clouds, and Skyress descended onto the field.

Skyress unfurled her wings and gave a chilling battle cry. She was a magnificent bird with wide wings and seven long tail-feathers. Her feet were sharp talons. A green jewel glowed on her forehead.

"What is that?" Runo asked in shock.

"Ventus Skyress!" Marucho said in awe. He had read about them, but had never seen one before.

"Ability Activate!" Shun cried out. "Winds of Fury!"

Skyress flapped her wings, and a strong wind whipped up. Tigrerra roared, trying to keep her balance as the winds lashed at her.

Skyress roared again, and the two Falconeer flew up behind her. They launched themselves at Tigrerra, slamming into her. She roared in protest.

"Tigrerra power decrease by one hundred Gs," the Baku-pod said.

"Oh no!" Marucho yelled.

"Come on, Tigrerra!" Runo called out. "You can't quit now!"

The Falconeers flew to Saurus.

Bam! They knocked him out of the battle in one blow.

Next, they turned to Limulus.

Bam! The Aquos Bakugan rolled back to Marucho's feet.

Tigrerra panted, exhausted.

"You've gotta get back in there," Runo pleaded with Tigrerra. "You can't lose!"

But Tigrerra was beat. "My battle is ended," she said.

She transformed back into a Bakugan ball.

The winds died down.

"Is it over?" Preyas asked.

Runo and Marucho stared at the three fallen Bakugan balls.

"Completely," Marucho said, defeated. "And that includes Limulus and Saurus! Shun's Winds of Fury attack knocked us out with one blow. Unreal!"

Runo put her hands on her knees, trying to take it all

in. With Tigrerra gone, they didn't stand a chance of winning!

Marucho thought quickly, trying to figure out how the attack worked. "He launched his Skyress last so his Falconeers could run interference," he muttered to himself. Then he ran up behind Runo. "Hey, Runo, I just figured it out!"

"Yeah, hang in there, Runo," Preyas added. "It's not over until the pleasantly plump lady sings."

"Yeah!" Marucho cheered.

Runo couldn't believe it. "You mean we still have a chance?"

Marucho nodded. "Now that we know his move, we can counter him and beat him!"

CHAPTER 12

RUNO AND MARUCHO'S LAST CHANCE

We need a surprise attack," Marucho said. He grabbed Preyas out of the air. "We need you, Preyas. You're our last hope!"

Preyas let out a scared yelp as Marucho hurled him onto the field.

"Bakugan Brawl!"

Preyas landed on the card with Shun's first Falconeer.

"Preyas Stand!" Marucho commanded.

Preyas burst from his ball. The Aquos Bakugan looked like a strange half-fish, half-human creature with blue scales all over his body. His mouth looked like a shark's jaws with rows of gleaming teeth. Preyas was a big jokester, too. He opened up a frilly red and white umbrella and twirled it around.

"I heard there's a little party happening and I thought I'd hop in and play!" he said in a sing-song voice. He turned to face Falconeer. "Shall we begin?"

Falconeer flew above the card, flapping his wings. Preyas's smirk turned to a look of panic.

"Now what do I do?" he cried.

Preyas at three hundred Gs. Falconeer remains stable at three hundred twenty Gs, said the Baku-pod.

Marucho frowned. "This doesn't look good."

"Don't worry, Marucho," Runo said confidently. "I've got it all figured out."

"You sure you know what you're doing?" Marucho asked.

"I have to get Tigrerra into the battle to help Preyas," Runo replied.

That didn't make Marucho feel any better. "But Runo, once a Bakugan loses in a battle, the rules clearly state you can't use it again!"

"Yeah, but I think I found a loophole," Runo told him. "Just leave it to me, 'kay? But here's what you can do. You keep Shun's Skyress busy with Preyas."

Marucho nervously rifled through his remaining cards. "Yeah, sure . . ."

"Are you ready?" Shun called out. He sounded tough. "Gate Card Open!"

The Gate Card underneath the two Bakugan flipped over. "Positive Delta!" Shun cried.

"You've got to be kidding!" Marucho said. He knew what that card could do.

Rays of light shot up underneath Preyas's webbed feet.

"Oh crud!" he yelled. He jumped up. "Change of Attribute! Darkus!"

Preyas twirled around, bathed in blinding light.

"Change of Attribute! Darkus!" Preyas shouted.

When he set back down on the field, his entire body was purple.

"Ta-da!" Preyas cheered.

Shun looked confused. "What? Attribute Change? No way!"

Marucho grinned. His Preyas could change his attribute at will. It felt good to surprise Shun.

"Falconeer Power Reduction to one hundred twenty Gs."

"But how?" Runo asked.

"This is so cool," Marucho said with excitement. "Shun's Positive Delta steals power away from Water, Light, and Fire Attributes. But when it's attacked by Wind, Earth, and Darkus, it works in reverse! In other words, my Preyas is sapping Shun's Falconeer dry!"

Runo nodded, understanding. "Oh yeah! That's because Preyas changed his attribute."

"Way to go, Preyas!" Marucho called out. "That was sweet!"

"Yep, it's a dirty job, but somebody's got to do it," Preyas quipped. "All right. Incomiiiiiiiiiiiiiing!"

He jumped across the card, careening into Falconeer. The Ventus Bakugan turned back into a Bakugan ball and rolled back to Shun.

Shun calmly caught it. "So . . . there is a Bakugan who can change his own attribute," he said thoughtfully.

He tossed Skyress back out onto an empty Gate Card.

"Skyress enters battle," announced the Baku-pod.

"Whoa!" Runo cried. "Okay, Griffon. Brawl!"

There was still one Falconeer left on the field. Runo threw a white Bakugan ball onto the card with it. A white Bakugan emerged. It had the head and body of a lion, the wings of an eagle, and a long, reptilian tail.

"Ability Card Activate!" Runo shouted. "Venomous Beast Torrent Attack!"

Griffon began to glow. In the next instant, he transformed. Now Tigrerra faced Falconeer!

"Whoa," Shun said, impressed.

Tigrerra roared and attacked Falconeer with her sharp claws extended. Falconeer turned back into a Bakugan ball.

Tigrerra turned back into a ball, too, and bounced back into Runo's hand.

"Nice job!" Runo told Tigrerra.

"Thank you for giving me a second chance," the Bakugan said proudly.

"I didn't realize you could morph your Bakugan," Marucho said. "That's how you got Tigrerra into the battle again."

"Ah, let's talk about that later, Marucho," Runo said. "We still have one more battle to win."

Shun was down to one Bakugan. Runo still had Tigrerra, and Marucho had Preyas. If one of them could take down Shun's Skyress, Runo and Marucho would win the battle.

"Bakugan Brawl!" Marucho yelled. He tossed Preyas onto the card with Skyress. "Preyas Stand!"

Preyas exploded onto the card as Marucho quickly made his next move.

"Ability Card Activate! Wind and Water Combine!"

Runo threw Tigrerra onto the card with Preyas. "Ability Card Activate! Savage Edge!"

Preyas jumped on Tigrerra's back. Now they could fight with the combined power of their Gs.

Shun's eyes gleamed. "Gate Card Open!"

The card flipped over.

"Accessing strength," said the Baku-pod. "Skyress Power Surge to seven hundred twenty Gs. Preyas increase to four hundred Gs. Tigrerra to three hundred forty Gs."

The Gate Card gave them all a boost of power — but the biggest boost went to Skyress, a Ventus Bakugan. Still, it wasn't enough to beat Runo and Marucho.

"Once you add that up we're at seven hundred and forty Gs!" Runo said happily.

Preyas rocked back and forth on Tigrerra's back. "We are the champions! We are the champions!"

Tigrerra was all business. "Let's finish this!" she roared.

She lunged at Skyress, knocking her down.

"Shun!" Skyress cried.

"Don't worry, Skyress," he said. He held up a card. "I still haven't played my ace yet! Ability Card Activate! Fire Storm!"

"*Skyress Power Increase detected,*" reported the Baku-pod. "Combined reading at nine hundred and twenty Gs."

Marucho gasped. He had never seen one Bakugan with so much power!

"We're in trouble!" Preyas said.

Skyress floated up over the field. Green and blue flames burned all over her body. Her eyes glowed with heat.

With a shriek, she dove at Tigrerra and Preyas.

SLAM!

The two Bakugan went hurling backward. They transformed back into Bakugan balls as the field vanished around them.

Shun caught Skyress's Bakugan ball.

"Game over," he said calmly. "You lose our bet."

"B-but . . ." Marucho couldn't believe it.

Shun won the battle. Now he wouldn't join their team.

Without Shun, they couldn't beat Masquerade.

Would all of their Bakugan be destined for the Doom Dimension?

Runo was shocked. "Oh, no," she said quietly.

This couldn't be over — it just couldn't!

WARRIOR CLASSES

In the alternate dimension called Vestroia, Bakugan warriors live on six different worlds. There are many different classes of warriors, and new ones are being discovered. On these pages you'll meet some of these beastly brawlers. Look for more in the next Bakugan book!

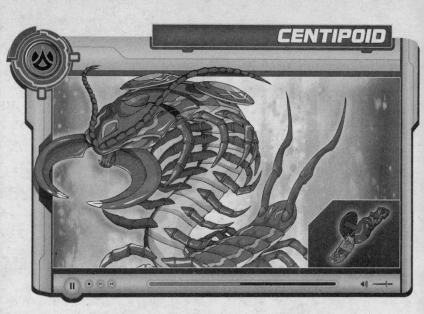

CENTIPOID

CENTIPOID

For some people, the sight of a tiny centipede, with all those wiggling legs, is enough to make their skin crawl. Now imagine a centipede as big as a bus. That's Centipoid! Using this big bug in battle is sure to bug your opponents.

FEAR RIPPER

FEAR RIPPER

When this frightening Bakugan appears on the field, opponents shiver with fear. That's because this creepy creature has sharp blades instead of hands, and is known for its fierce and ferocious attacks.

GARGONOID

GARGONOID

If you've ever seen a gargoyle, you know what
Gargonoid looks like. This Bakugan looks a lot like
one of these old stone statues, with its monstrous face
and leathery wings. But there's one difference:
Gargonoid doesn't just sit around and stare. This
Bakugan really knows how to pound its opponents.

GRIFFON

This Bakugan looks like a mythical beast. It has the
body of a lion, the wings of an eagle, and the tail of a
reptile. But Griffon is not something out of a fairy
tale. When this Bakugan attacks, you know it's real!

HYNOID

HYNOID

Hynoid doesn't need a full moon to unleash his fury.
This werewolflike Bakugan is ready to rumble no
matter what is shining up in the sky. Part hyena, this
Bakugan has sharp claws, powerful limbs, and a bad
attitude.

LIMULUS

LIMULUS

Limulus looks like something you'd find on the beach.
It has a hard, armored shell like a horseshoe crab.
Spikes on top of the shell add extra defensive power.
When it's attacked, Limulus lashes out with two long,
strong tentacles.

RATTLEOID

RATTLEOID

Let's face it — snakes are scary. Rattleoid is a *giant* snake, with long, sharp fangs and a rattle on the end of its tail. Armor on top of its head gives Rattleoid extra protection from attackers.

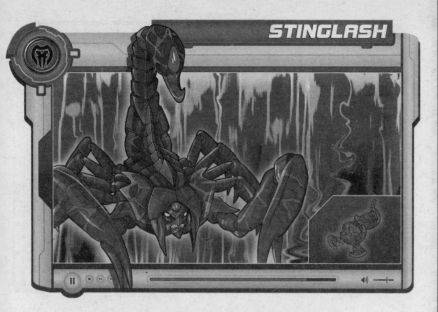

STINGLASH

This Bakugan looks like a scorpion with a human face. And Stinglash has more going for it than just scary looks. When it attacks, Stinglash lashes out with its super-sharp stinger.

TERRORCLAW

Watch out for those claws! This crabby Bakugan has sharp, snapping pincers that can tear an opponent to shreds.

TUSKOR

This big Bakugan looks like a mammoth, a huge elephant with long tusks. Tuskor can crush its opponents with its massive feet. With the Ability Card, Nose Slap, Tuskor can attack a Bakugan on a different card.

WORMQUAKE

WORMQUAKE

This gigantic worm has no face, just a wide open mouth filled with sharp teeth. Wormquake can burrow into the ground, causing it to shake like an earthquake.